Y0-CJE-994

One day Jacob and his brother Jonathan went into a forest. They had a map that led them to magical crystals. Little did they know that the forest was also the same place where the deadly dragon roamed. Suddenly, the dragon appeared out of nowhere and swooped up Jacob and Jonathan!

They were both thrown into a portal by the deadly dragon. Jacob and Jonathan found themselves falling from the sky into the hot desert. They landed with a big boom. They got up, not feeling well, and they started walking slowly towards a village that they saw from a distance. They felt lost, dazed, and had a little belly ache.

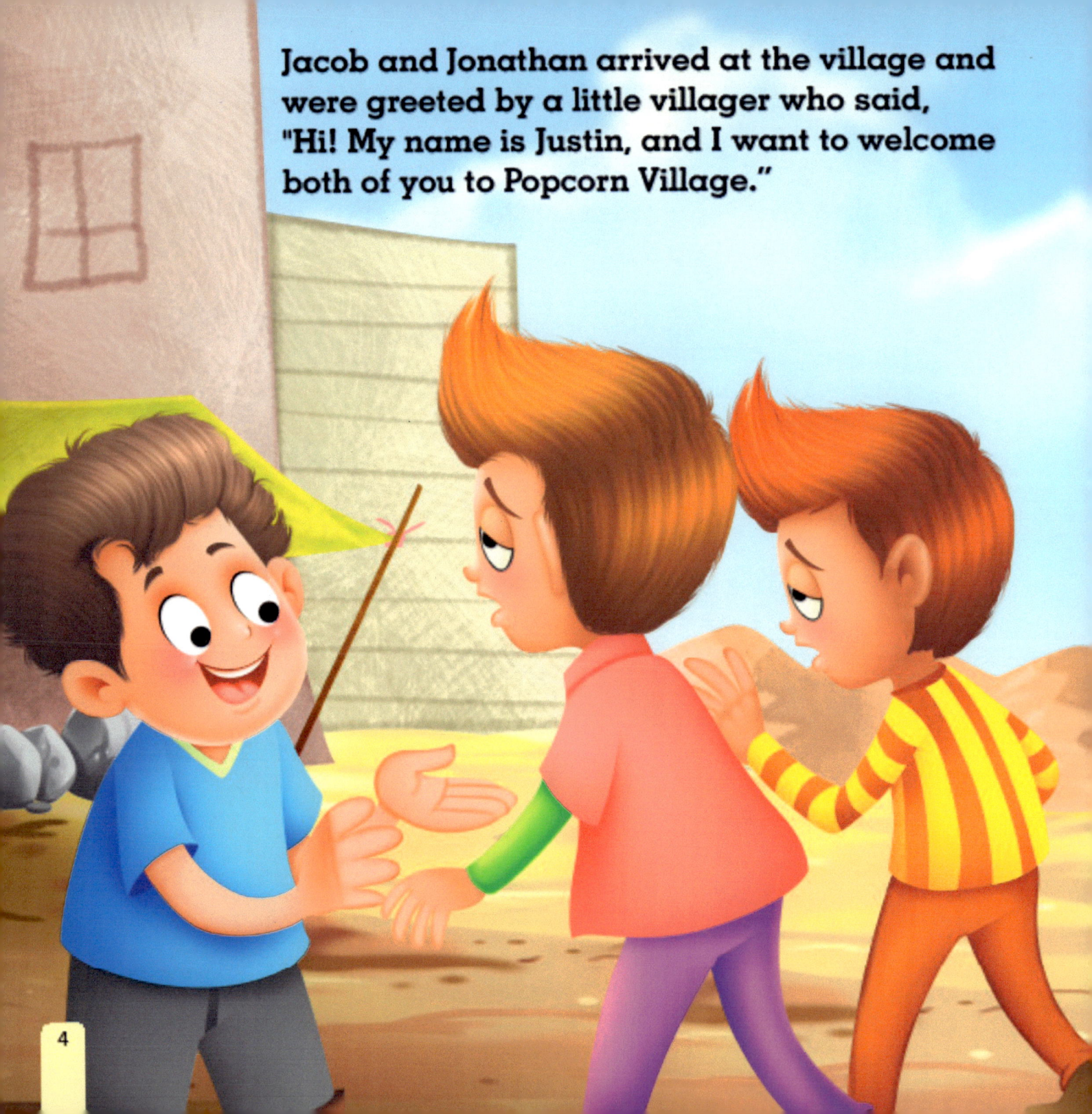

Jacob and Jonathan arrived at the village and were greeted by a little villager who said, "Hi! My name is Justin, and I want to welcome both of you to Popcorn Village."

Jacob responded by explaining to Justin how he and Jonathan were swooped up by the deadly dragon, thrown into the portal, and how they got to the village. Jacob also told Justin how they landed on their bellies and how their bellies hurt a little bit from the fall.

Jacob and Jonathan then asked Justin if he knew of any cures for the tummy aches. Justin took a water bottle that was in his back pocket out and handed it to Jonathan and Jacob.

Jacob drank the water, made one loud burp, and felt instantly better. Jonathan drank some water as well, and burped five times louder. The sound of the burp was as loud as a whale.

Now that Jonathan was feelings better, he asked why the village is called Popcorn Village. Justin replied that his village makes the world's best popcorn. Jacob asked, "How do you make the world's best popcorn?" Justin responded that it is top secret. Justin then told Jacob and Jonathan that the popcorn has special powers that will help them get back home.

Justin led Jacob and Jonathan back to the portal so they can **return** back to the forest. He then gave Jacob and Jonathan a bag each of the world's best popcorn. Jonathan and Jacob said thank you and good-bye to Justin as they jumped into the portal.

When they arrived back in the forest into the land of dragons, they were greeted by a horrible smell.

Jacob thought it was the dragon's poo poo but Jonathan thought it was the dragon's bad breath. However, they were both greeted by the deadly dragon's fire-breathing mouth.

Jacob and Jonathan ran away quickly from the dragon and fled into the mines. Jacob had heard the tale from his friend Carter that there were super magical crystals in the mines in the forest.

These super magical crystals had special powers. Upon touching these crystals, you could defeat any dragon. While in the mines Jacob saw a crystal and reached out to pick up a crystal, but it was a fake crystal, so nothing happened. Jonathan picked up another crystal, and again, nothing happened.

While Jacob and Jonathan walked further into the forest, they noticed that there were dynamites planted everywhere in the mines. Jonathan gave Jacob a distressed look. Jonathan and Jacob tried to move slowly and cautiously out of the mines, but it was too late. The explosives started going off with big loud booms!

A research team nearby had heard the loud explosions came running to see what had happened. They had dogs with them that sniffed out the popcorn that Jonathan and Jacob were still carrying. The dogs alerted the researchers to the two boys they had found.

Jacob and Jonathan told the researchers they were trying to get away from a deadly dragon, and they were trying to locate the magical crystals to defeat the dragon. They asked the researchers if they have seen such crystals. The researchers said no, and had not even heard of such magical crystals.

Just as brothers were asking the researchers these questions, the deadly dragon appeared. The dragon had smelled the magical popcorn and wanted the magical popcorn bag.

The dragon fired a great deal of smoke from it's nostrils and said, "Give me that popcorn!" Jacob and Jonathan refused and ran away.

A few moments later, Jacob said, "Maybe we should taste the magical popcorn and see how it can help us to get back home. Jonathan said, "OK! Maybe a little bit." Jonathan opened the popcorn to taste some. As he tasted the popcorn he suddenly started to fly. Jonathan said, "Look Jacob I can fly." Jacob opened his bag and tasted a little of his popcorn. Suddenly, Jacob also started to fly as well.

As Jacob was flying in the sky he said to Jonathan, "Wow I can see the ground and inside the tree from here." Jacob said, "I can also see the ground as well from here but let's fly down to the ground and see if we can find the magical crystals to defeat the dragon and fly back home."

As they continued moving through the forest, Jacob said, "Look, Jonathan, I can see something glowing next to the bush." "Let's go and check it out."

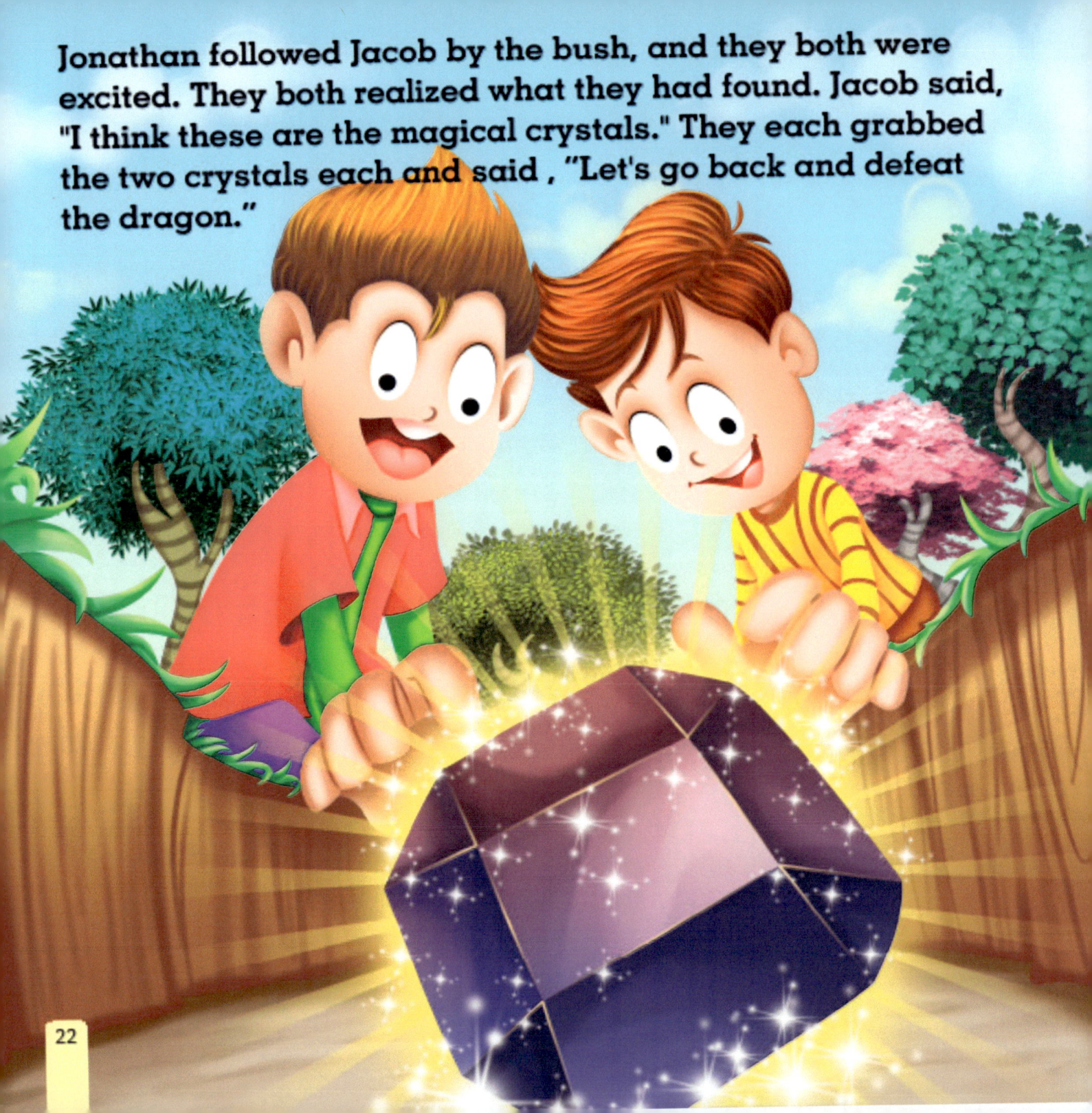

Jonathan followed Jacob by the bush, and they both were excited. They both realized what they had found. Jacob said, "I think these are the magical crystals." They each grabbed the two crystals each and said , "Let's go back and defeat the dragon."

They walked back and found the deadly dragon. Jonathan said, "Hi, Mr. Dragon, we want to share our popcorn with you." The dragon said, "I want both of your magical popcorn bag." I want to be the most powerful dragon in the forest."

Just as the dragon was speaking, Jacob took his magical crystals and threw them at the dragon. Just as the magical crystals hit the dragon, the deadly dragon disappeared into thin air.

Jacob and Jonathan yelled, "We did it! We defeated the dragon!" Jacob told Jonathan that Carter was right. Jacob and Jonathan took their popcorn bag and magical crystals. Then they both flew back home.